THE REAL
MOTHER GOOSE

SEE-SAW

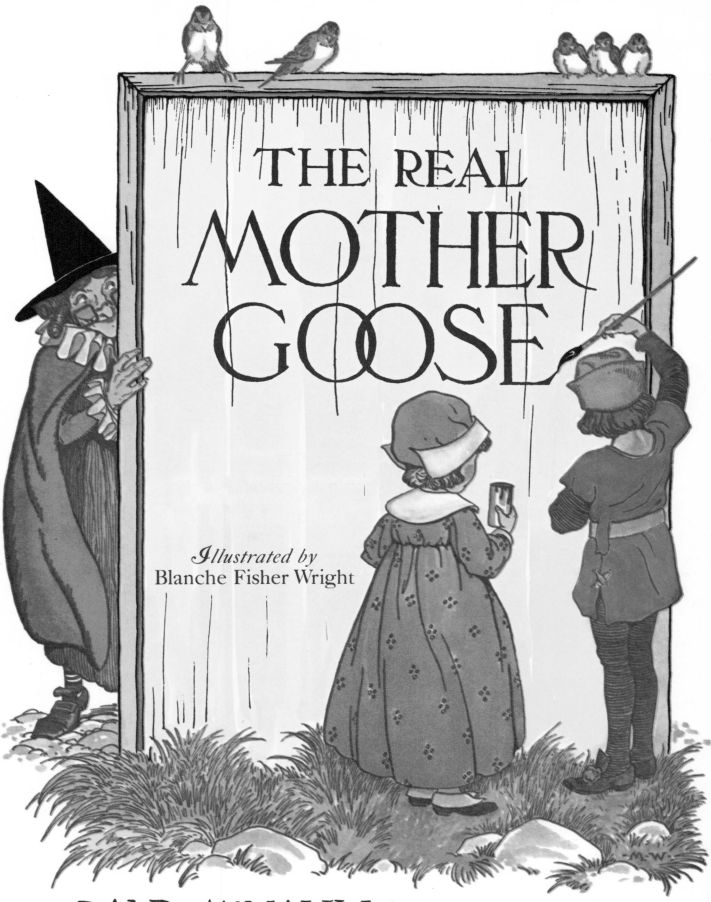

THE REAL MOTHER GOOSE

Illustrated by
Blanche Fisher Wright

RAND McNALLY & CO. CHICAGO

Printed in U. S. A.

First printing, 1916
Second printing, 1917
Third printing, 1918
Fourth printing, 1919
Fifth printng, 1920
Sixth printing, 1921
Seventh printing, 1922
Eighth printing, 1923
Ninth printing, 1924
Tenth printing, 1925
Eleventh printing, 1926
Twelfth printing, 1927
Thirteenth printing, 1928
Fourteenth printing, 1930
Fifteenth printing, 1931
Sixteenth printing, 1932
Seventeenth printing, July, 1934
Eighteenth printing, April, 1935
Nineteenth printing, September, 1936
Twentieth printing, December, 1938
Twenty-first printing, March, 1940
Twenty-second printing, February, 1941
Twenty-third printing, August, 1941
Twenty-fourth printing, August, 1942
Twenty-fifth printing, January, 1943
Twenty-sixth printing, March, 1944
Twenty-seventh printing, November, 1944
Twenty-eighth printing, June, 1945
Twenty-ninth printing, December, 1945
Thirtieth printing, June, 1946
Thirty-first printing, May, 1948
Thirty-second printing, January, 1950
Thirty-third printing, March, 1951
Thirty-fourth printing, January, 1952
Thirty-fifth printing, December, 1952
Thirty-sixth printing, December, 1953
Thirty-seventh printing, December, 1954
Thirty-eighth printing, October, 1956
Thirty-ninth printing, May, 1957
Fortieth printing, October, 1958
Forty-first printing, June, 1960
Forty-second printing, January, 1961
Forty-third printing, January, 1962
Forty-fourth printing, Febuary, 1963
Forty-fifth printing, October, 1963
Forty-sixth printing, May, 1964
Forty-seventh printing, January, 1965
Forty-eighth printing, September, 1965
Forty-ninth printing, April, 1966
Fiftieth printing, May, 1966
Fifty-first printing, July, 1967
Fifty-second printing, May, 1968
Fifty-third printing, July, 1969
Fifty-fourth printing, August, 1970
Fifty-fifth printing, July, 1971
Fifty-sixth printing, October, 1971
Fifty-seventh printing, October, 1972
Fifty-eighth printing, January, 1973
Fifty-ninth printing, October, 1973
Sixtieth printing, March, 1974
Sixty-first printing, July, 1974
Sixty-second printing, November, 1974
Sixty-third printing, July, 1975

A LIST OF THE RHYMES

(For an alphabetical list of first lines see pp. 7-9)

AN ALPHABETICAL LIST OF FIRST LINES

7

RAIN

THE REAL
MOTHER GOOSE

LITTLE BO-PEEP

Little Bo-Peep has lost her sheep,
    And can't tell where to find
       them;
Leave them alone, and they'll come
       home,
    And bring their tails behind
       them.

Little Bo-Peep fell fast asleep,
    And dreamt she heard them
       bleating;
But when she awoke, she found it
    a joke,
    For still they all were fleeting.

Then up she took her little crook,
    Determined for to find them;
She found them indeed, but it made
    her heart bleed,
    For they'd left all their tails
       behind 'em!

It happened one day, as Bo-peep
    did stray
    Unto a meadow hard by—

There she espied their tails, side
    by side,
    All hung on a tree to dry.

She heaved a sigh and wiped her eye,
    And over the hillocks she
       raced;
And tried what she could, as a
       shepherdess should,
    That each tail should be prop-
       erly placed.

LITTLE BOY BLUE

Little Boy Blue, come, blow your
    horn!
The sheep's in the meadow, the
    cow's in the corn.
Where's the little boy that looks
    after the sheep?
Under the haystack, fast asleep!

RAIN

Rain, rain, go away,
Come again another day;
Little Johnny wants to play.

FINGERS AND TOES

Every lady in this land
Has twenty nails, upon each
hand
Five, and twenty on hands and
feet:
All this is true, without deceit.

A SEASONABLE SONG

Piping hot, smoking hot.
What I've got
You have not.
Hot gray pease, hot, hot, hot;
Hot gray pease, hot.

THE CLOCK

There's a neat little clock,—
In the schoolroom it stands,—
And it points to the time
With its two little hands.

And may we, like the clock,
Keep a face clean and bright,
With hands ever ready
To do what is right.

WINTER

Cold and raw the north wind
doth blow,
Bleak in the morning early;
All the hills are covered with
snow,
And winter's now come fairly.

DAME TROT AND HER CAT

Dame Trot and her cat
  Led a peaceable life,
When they were not troubled
  With other folks' strife.

When Dame had her dinner
  Pussy would wait,
And was sure to receive
  A nice piece from her plate.

THREE CHILDREN ON THE ICE

Three children sliding on the ice
  Upon a summer's day,
As it fell out, they all fell in,
  The rest they ran away.

Oh, had these children been at
    school,
  Or sliding on dry ground,
Ten thousand pounds to one penny
  They had not then been drowned.

Ye parents who have children dear,
  And ye, too, who have none,
If you would keep them safe abroad
  Pray keep them safe at home.

CROSS PATCH

Cross patch, draw the latch,
  Sit by the fire and spin;
Take a cup and drink it up,
  Then call your neighbors in.

THE OLD WOMAN UNDER A HILL

There was an old woman
  Lived under a hill;
And if she's not gone,
  She lives there still.

TWEEDLE-DUM AND TWEEDLE-DEE

Tweedle-dum and Tweedle-dee
  Resolved to have a battle,
For Tweedle-dum said Tweedle-dee
  Had spoiled his nice new rattle.

Just then flew by a monstrous crow,
  As big as a tar barrel,
Which frightened both the heroes so,
  They quite forgot their quarrel.

OH, DEAR!

Dear, dear! what can the matter be?
Two old women got up in an apple-
tree;
One came down, and the other
stayed till Saturday.

OLD MOTHER GOOSE

Old Mother Goose, when
    She wanted to wander,
Would ride through the air
    On a very fine gander.

LITTLE JUMPING JOAN

Here am I, little jumping Joan,
When nobody's with me
    I'm always alone.

PAT-A-CAKE

Pat-a-cake, pat-a-cake,
    Baker's man!
So I do, master,
    As fast as I can.

Pat it, and prick it,
    And mark it with T,
Put it in the oven
    For Tommy and me.

MONEY AND THE MARE

"Lend me thy mare to ride a mile."
"She is lamed, leaping over a stile."

"Alack! and I must keep the fair!
I'll give thee money for thy mare."

"Oh, oh! say you so?
Money will make the mare to go!"

ROBIN REDBREAST

Little Robin Redbreast sat upon a tree
Up went Pussy-Cat, down went he,
Down came Pussy-Cat, away Robin
    ran,
Says little Robin Redbreast: "Catch
    me if you can!"

Little Robin Redbreast jumped upon
    a spade,
Pussy-Cat jumped after him, and
    then he was afraid.
Little Robin chirped and sang, and
    what did Pussy say?
Pussy-Cat said: "Mew, mew, mew,
    and Robin flew away.

PAT-A-CAKE

A MELANCHOLY SONG

Trip upon trenchers,
And dance upon dishes,
My mother sent me for some barm,
    some barm;
She bid me go lightly,
And come again quickly,
For fear the young men should do
    me some harm.
Yet did n't you see, yet did n't you
    see,
What naughty tricks they put upon
    me?

They broke my
    pitcher
And spilt the
    water,
And huffed my
    mother,
And chid her
    daughter,
And kissed my
    sister instead
    of me.

JACK

Jack be nimble, Jack be
    quick,
Jack jump over the candle-
    stick.

GOING TO ST. IVES

As I was going to St. Ives
I met a man with seven wives.
Every wife had seven sacks,
Every sack had seven cats,
Every cat had seven kits.
Kits, cats, sacks, and wives,
How many were going to St. Ives

BEES

A swarm of bees in May
Is worth a load of hay;
A swarm of bees in June
Is worth a silver spoon;
A swarm of bees in July
Is not worth a fly.

COME OUT TO PLAY

Girls and boys, come out to play,
The moon doth shine as bright as
  day;
Leave your supper, and leave your
  sleep,
And come with your playfellows
  into the street.
Come with a whoop, come with a
  call,
Come with a good will or not at all.
Up the ladder and down the wall,
A half-penny roll will serve us all.
You find milk, and I'll find flour,
And we'll have a pudding in half
  an hour.

THIRTY DAYS HATH
SEPTEMBER

Thirty days hath September,
April, June, and November;
February has twenty-eight alone,
All the rest have thirty-one,
Excepting leap-year, that's the time
When February's days are twenty-
  nine.

BABY DOLLY

Hush, baby, my dolly, I pray you
  don't cry,
And I'll give you some bread, and
  some milk by-and-by;
Or perhaps you like custard, or,
  maybe, a tart,
Then to either you're welcome, with
  all my heart.

TO MARKET, TO MARKET, TO BUY A FAT PIG

IF WISHES WERE HORSES

If wishes were horses, beggars would
ride.
If turnips were watches, I would
wear one by my side.
And if "ifs" and "ands"
Were pots and pans,
There'd be no work for tinkers!

TO MARKET

To market, to market, to buy a fat
pig,
Home again, home again, jiggety jig.
To market, to market, to buy a fat
hog,
Home again, home again, jiggety
jog.
To market, to market, to buy a plum
bun,
Home again, home again, market is
done.

OLD CHAIRS TO MEND

If I'd as much money as I could
spend,
I never would cry old chairs to
mend;
Old chairs to mend, old chairs to
mend;
I never would cry old chairs to mend.

If I'd as much money as I could
tell,
I never would cry old clothes to
sell;
Old clothes to sell, old clothes to
sell;
I never would cry old clothes to sell.

ROBIN AND RICHARD

Robin and Richard were two pretty men,
They lay in bed till the clock struck ten;
Then up starts Robin and looks at the sky,
"Oh, brother Richard, the sun's very high!
You go before, with the bottle and bag,
And I will come after on little Jack Nag."

A MAN AND A MAID

There was a little man,
Who wooed a little maid,
And he said, "Little maid, will you
    wed, wed, wed?
I have little more to say,
So will you, yea or nay,
For least said is soonest mended-ded,
    ded, ded."

The little maid replied,
"Should I be your little bride,
Pray what must we have for to eat,
    eat, eat?
Will the flame that you're so
    rich in
Light a fire in the kitchen?
Or the little god of love turn the
    spit, spit, spit?"

HERE GOES MY LORD

Here goes my lord
A trot, a trot, a trot, a trot,
Here goes my lady
A canter, a canter, a canter, a canter!

Here goes my young master
Jockey-hitch, jockey-hitch, jockey-
    hitch, jockey-hitch!
Here goes my young miss
An amble, an amble, an amble, an
    amble!

The footman lags behind to tipple
    ale and wine,
And goes gallop, a gallop, a gallop,
    to make up his time.

THE CLEVER HEN

I had a little hen, the prettiest
    ever seen,
She washed me the dishes and
    kept the house clean;
She went to the mill to fetch me
    some flour,
She brought it home in less than
    an hour;
She baked me my bread, she
    brewed me my ale,
She sat by the fire and told
    many a fine tale.

LUCY LOCKET

TWO BIRDS

There were two birds sat on a stone,
    Fa, la, la, la, lal, de;
One flew away, and then there was
    one,
    Fa, la, la, la, lal, de;
The other bird flew after,
And then there was none,
    Fa, la, la, la, lal, de;
And so the stone
Was left alone,
    Fa, la, la, la, lal, de.

LEG OVER LEG

Leg over leg,
As the dog went to Dover;
When he came to a stile,
Jump, he went over.

LUCY LOCKET

Lucy Locket lost her pocket,
Kitty Fisher found it;
Nothing in it, nothing in it,
But the binding round it.

WHEN JENNY WREN
WAS YOUNG

'Twas once upon a time, when
    Jenny Wren was young,
So daintily she danced and so pret-
    tily she sung,
Robin Redbreast lost his heart, for
    he was a gallant bird.
So he doffed his hat to Jenny Wren,
    requesting to be heard.

"Oh, dearest Jenny Wren, if you
    will but be mine,
You shall feed on cherry pie and
    drink new currant wine,
I'll dress you like a goldfinch or any
    peacock gay,
So, dearest Jen, if you'll be mine, let
    us appoint the day."

Jenny blushed behind her fan and
    thus declared her mind:
"Since, dearest Bob, I love you well,
    I'll take your offer kind.
Cherry pie is very nice and so is
    currant wine,
But I must wear my plain brown
    gown and never go too fine."

SOLOMON GRUNDY

Solomon Grundy,
Born on a Monday,
Christened on Tuesday,
Married on Wednesday,
Took ill on Thursday,
Worse on Friday,
Died on Saturday,
Buried on Sunday.
This is the end
Of Solomon Grundy.

BARBER

Barber, barber, shave a pig.
How many hairs will make a wig?
Four and twenty; that's enough.
Give the barber a pinch of snuff.

THE FLYING PIG

Dickory, dickory, dare,
The pig flew up in the air;
The man in brown soon brought
     him down,
       Dickory,
         dickory,
          dare.

HUSH-A-BYE

Hush-a-bye, baby, on the tree top!
When the wind blows the cradle
    will rock;
When the bough breaks the cradle
    will fall;
Down will come baby, bough, cradle
    and all.

BURNIE BEE

Burnie bee, burnie bee,
Tell me when your wedding be?
If it be to-morrow day,
Take your wings and fly away.

THREE WISE MEN OF GOTHAM

Three wise men of Gotham
Went to sea in a bowl;
If the bowl had been stronger
My song had been longer.

THE HUNTER OF REIGATE

A man went a-hunting at Reigate,
And wished to leap over a high
    gate.
Says the owner, "Go round,
With your gun and your hound,
For you never shall leap over my
    gate."

PIPPEN HILL

As I was going up Pippen Hill,
　　Pippen Hill was dirty;
There I met a pretty Miss,
　　And she dropped me a
　　　　curtsy.

Little Miss, pretty Miss,
　　Blessings light upon you;
If I had half-a-crown a day,
　　I'd spend it all upon you.

LITTLE POLLY FLINDERS

Little Polly Flinders
Sat among the cinders
　　Warming her pretty little toes;
Her mother came and caught her,
Whipped her little daughter
　　For spoiling her nice new
　　　　clothes.

RIDE AWAY, RIDE AWAY

Ride away, ride away,
　　Johnny shall ride,
And he shall have pussy-cat
　　Tied to one side;
And he shall have little dog
　　Tied to the other,
And Johnny shall ride
　　To see his grandmother.

PUSSY-CAT AND QUEEN

"Pussy-cat, pussy-cat,
　　Where have you been?"
"I've been to London
　　To look at the Queen."

"Pussy-cat, pussy-cat,
　　What did you there?"
"I frightened a little mouse
　　Under the chair."

THE WINDS

Mister East gave a feast;
Mister North laid the cloth;
Mister West did his best;
Mister South burnt his mouth
Eating cold potato.

PUSSY-CAT AND QUEEN

ELIZABETH

Elizabeth,   Elspeth,   Betsy,   and
    Bess,

They all went together to seek a
    bird's nest;

They found a bird's nest with five
    eggs in,

They all took one, and left four in.

JUST LIKE ME

"I went up one pair of stairs."
    "Just like me."

"I went up two pairs of stairs."
    "Just like me."

"I went into a room."
    "Just like me."

"I looked out of a window."
    "Just like me."

"And there I saw a monkey."
    "Just like me."

CLAP HANDIES

Clap, clap handies,

Mammie's wee, wee ain;

Clap, clap handies,

Daddie's comin' hame,

Hame till his bonny wee bit laddie;

Clap, clap handies,

My wee, wee ain.

CHRISTMAS

Christmas comes but once a year,

And when it comes it brings good
    cheer.

PLAY DAYS

How many days has my baby to
    play?

Saturday, Sunday, Monday,

Tuesday, Wednesday, Thursday,
    Friday,

Saturday, Sunday, Monday.

HEIGH-HO, THE CARRION CROW

A carrion crow sat on an oak,
    Fol de riddle, lol de riddle,
      hi ding do,
Watching a tailor shape his
    cloak;
    Sing heigh-ho, the carrion
      crow,
    Fol de riddle, lol de riddle,
      hi ding do!

Wife, bring me my old bent bow,
    Fol de riddle, lol de riddle,
      hi ding do,
That I may shoot yon carrion
    crow;
    Sing heigh-ho, the carrion
      crow,
    Fol de riddle, lol de riddle,
      hi ding do!

The tailor he shot, and missed
    his mark,
    Fol de riddle, lol de riddle,
      hi ding do!
And shot his own sow quite
    through the heart;
    Sing heigh-ho, the carrion crow,
    Fol de riddle, lol de riddle,
      hi ding do!

Wife! bring brandy in a spoon,
    Fol de riddle, lol de riddle,
      hi ding do!
For our old sow is in a swoon;
    Sing heigh-ho, the carrion
      crow,
    Fol de riddle, lol de riddle,
      hi ding do!

A B C

Great A, little a,
    Bouncing B!
The cat's in the cupboard,
    And can't see me.

A NEEDLE AND THREAD

Old Mother Twitchett had but
    one eye,
And a long tail which she let fly;
And every time she went through
    a gap,
A bit of her tail she left in a trap.

BANBURY CROSS

Ride a cock-horse to Banbury Cross,
To see an old lady upon a white
    horse.
Rings on her fingers, and bells on
    her toes,
She shall have music wherever she
    goes.

THE MAN IN OUR TOWN

There was a man in our town,
    And he was wondrous wise,
He jumped into a bramble bush,
    And scratched out both his
    eyes;
But when he saw his eyes were out,
    With all his might and main,
He jumped into another bush,
    And scratched 'em in again.

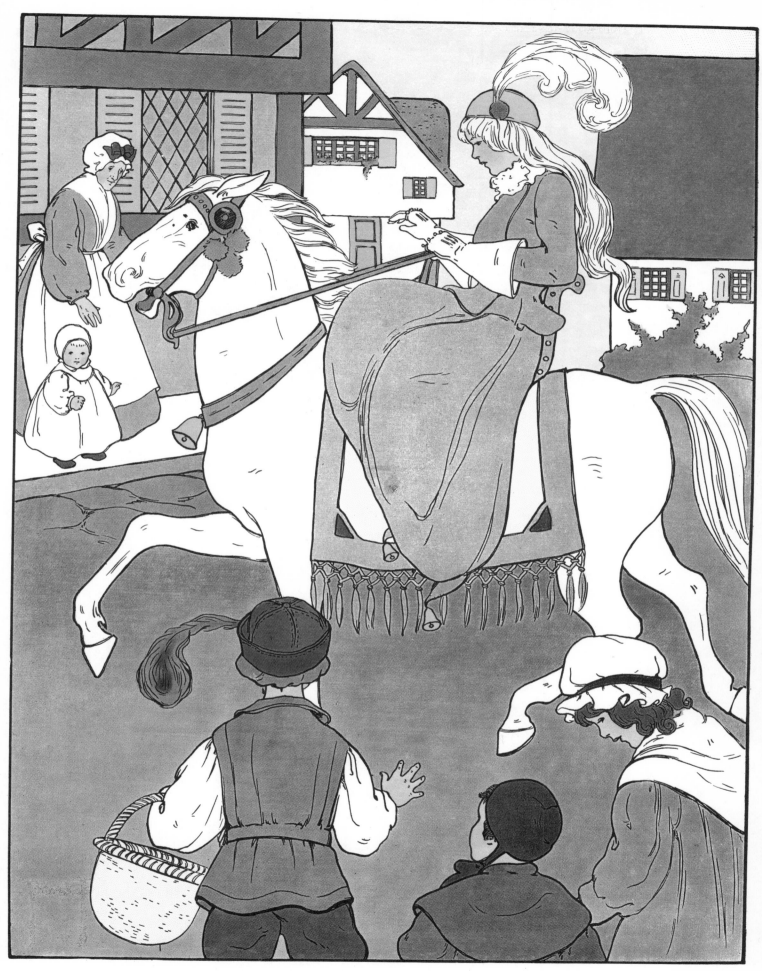

RIDE A COCK-HORSE TO BANBURY CROSS

GEORGY PORGY

Georgy Porgy, pudding and pie,
Kissed the girls and made them cry.
When the boys came out to play,
Georgy Porgy ran away.

FOR EVERY EVIL

For every evil under the sun
There is a remedy or there is none.
If there be one, seek till you find it;
If there be none, never mind it.

CUSHY COW

Cushy cow, bonny, let down thy milk,
And I will give thee a gown of silk;
A gown of silk and a silver tee,
If thou wilt let down thy milk to me.

WEE WILLIE WINKIE

Wee Willie Winkie runs through
    the town,
Upstairs and downstairs, in his
    nightgown;
Rapping at the window, crying
    through the lock,
"Are the children in their beds?
    Now it's eight o'clock."

ABOUT THE BUSH

About the bush, Willie,
    About the beehive,
About the bush, Willie,
    I'll meet thee alive.

SEE-SAW

See-saw, Margery Daw,
Sold her bed and lay upon straw.

ROBIN-A-BOBBIN

Robin-a-Bobbin
    Bent his bow,
Shot at a pigeon,
    And killed a crow.

JOHN SMITH

Is John Smith within?
Yes, that he is.
Can he set a shoe?
Ay, marry, two.
Here a nail, there a nail,
Tick, tack, too.

THREE BLIND MICE

SIMPLE SIMON

Simple Simon met a pieman,
    Going to the fair;
Says Simple Simon to the pieman,
    "Let me taste your ware."

Says the pieman to Simple Simon,
    "Show me first your penny,"
Says Simple Simon to the pieman,
    "Indeed, I have not any."

Simple Simon went a-fishing
    For to catch a whale;
All the water he could find
    Was in his mother's pail!

Simple Simon went to look
    If plums grew on a thistle;
He pricked his fingers very much,
    Which made poor Simon
        whistle.

He went to catch a dicky bird,
    And thought he could not fail,
Because he had a little salt,
    To put upon its tail.

He went for water with a sieve,
    But soon it ran all through;
And now poor Simple Simon
    Bids you all adieu.

THREE BLIND MICE

Three blind mice! See how they run!
They all ran after the farmer's wife,
Who cut off their tails with a carv-
    ing knife.
Did you ever see such a thing in
    your life
As three blind mice?

FIVE TOES

This little pig went to market;
This little pig stayed at home;
This little pig had roast beef;
This little pig had none;
This little pig said, "Wee, wee!
I can't find my way home."

The drake was a-swimming with
  his curly tail;
  The little man made it his mark,
  mark, mark.
He let off his gun, but he fired
  too soon,
  And the drake flew away with a
  quack, quack, quack.

DOCTOR FOSTER

Doctor Foster went to Glo'ster,
  In a shower of rain;
He stepped in a puddle, up to his
  middle,
  And never went there again.

A LITTLE MAN

There was a little man, and he had
  a little gun,
  And his bullets were made of
  lead, lead, lead;
He went to the brook, and saw a
  little duck,
  And shot it right through the
  head, head, head.

He carried it home to his old wife
  Joan,
  And bade her a fire to make,
  make, make.
To roast the little duck he had shot
  in the brook,
  And he'd go and fetch the drake,
  drake, drake.

DIDDLE DIDDLE DUMPLING

Diddle diddle dumpling, my son John
Went to bed with his breeches on,
One stocking off, and one stocking on;
Diddle diddle dumpling, my son John.

JERRY HALL

Jerry Hall, he was so small,
A rat could eat him, hat and all.

LENGTHENING DAYS

As the days grow longer
The storms grow stronger.

CURLY-LOCKS, CURLY-LOCKS, WILT THOU BE MINE?

THE BLACK HEN

Hickety, pickety, my black hen,
She lays eggs for gentlemen;
Gentlemen come every day
To see what my black hen
doth lay.

THE MIST

A hill full, a hole full,
Yet you cannot catch a bowl full.

A CANDLE

Little Nanny Etticoat
In a white petticoat,
And a red nose;
The longer she stands
The shorter she grows.

MISS MUFFET

Little Miss Muffet
Sat on a tuffet,
Eating of curds and whey;
There came a big spider,
And sat down beside her,
And frightened Miss Muffet away.

CURLY-LOCKS

Curly-locks, Curly-locks, wilt thou be mine?
Thou shalt not wash the dishes, nor yet feed
the swine;
But sit on a cushion, and sew a fine seam,
And feed upon strawberries, sugar, and
cream.

HUMPTY DUMPTY

Humpty Dumpty sat on a wall,
Humpty Dumpty had a great fall;
All the King's horses, and all the King's men
Cannot put Humpty Dumpty together again.

ONE, TWO, THREE

One, two, three, four, five,
Once I caught a fish alive.
Six, seven, eight, nine, ten,
But I let it go again.
Why did you let it go?
Because it bit my finger so.
Which finger did it bite?
The little one upon the right.

THE DOVE AND THE WREN

The dove says coo, coo, what shall
    I do?
I can scarce maintain two.
Pooh, pooh! says the wren, I've got
    ten,
And keep them all like gentlemen.

MASTER I HAVE

Master I have, and I am his man,
    Gallop a dreary dun;
Master I have, and I am his man,
    And I'll get a wife as fast as
      I can;
With a heighty gaily gamberally,
    Higgledy piggledy, niggledy,
     niggledy,
    Gallop a dreary dun.

PINS

See a pin and pick it up,
All the day you'll have good luck.
See a pin and let it lay,
Bad luck you'll have all the day.

SHALL WE GO A-SHEARING?

"Old woman, old woman, shall we
    go a-shearing?"
"Speak a little louder, sir, I am
    very thick of hearing."
"Old woman, old woman, shall I
    kiss you dearly?"
"Thank you, kind sir, I hear you
    very clearly."

GOOSEY, GOOSEY, GANDER

GOOSEY, GOOSEY, GANDER

Goosey, goosey, gander,
  Whither dost thou wander?
Upstairs and downstairs
  And in my lady's chamber.

There I met an old man
  Who would n't say his prayers;
I took him by the left leg,
  And threw him down the stairs.

OLD MOTHER HUBBARD

Old Mother Hubbard
Went to the cupboard,
  To give her poor dog a bone;
But when she got there
The cupboard was bare,
  And so the poor dog had none.

She went to the baker's
  To buy him some bread;
When she came back
  The dog was dead.

She went to the undertaker's
  To buy him a coffin;
When she got back
  The dog was laughing.

She took a clean dish
  To get him some tripe;
When she came back
  He was smoking a pipe.

She went to the alehouse
  To get him some beer;
When she came back
  The dog sat in a chair.

She went to the tavern
  For white wine and red;
When she came back
  The dog stood on his head.

She went to the hatter's
  To buy him a hat;
When she came back
  He was feeding the cat.

She went to the barber's
  To buy him a wig;
When she came back
  He was dancing a jig.

She went to the fruiterer's
  To buy him some fruit;
When she came back
  He was playing the flute.

She went to the tailor's
  To buy him a coat;
When she came back
  He was riding a goat.

She went to the cobbler's
  To buy him some shoes;
When she came back
  He was reading the news.

She went to the sempster's
  To buy him some linen;
When she came back
  The dog was a-spinning.

She went to the hosier's
  To buy him some hose;
When she came back
  He was dressed in his clothes.

The dame made a curtsy,
  The dog made a bow;
The dame said, "Your servant,"
  The dog said, "Bow-wow."

THE COCK AND THE HEN

"Cock, cock, cock, cock,
  I've laid an egg,
  Am I to gang ba—are-foot?"

"Hen, hen, hen, hen,
  I've been up and down
  To every shop in town,
  And cannot find a shoe
  To fit your foot,
  If I'd crow my hea—art out."

BLUE BELL BOY

I had a little boy,
  And called him Blue Bell;
Gave him a little work,—
  He did it very well.

I bade him go upstairs
  To bring me a gold pin;
In coal scuttle fell he,
  Up to his little chin.

He went to the garden
  To pick a little sage;
He tumbled on his nose,
  And fell into a rage.

He went to the cellar
  To draw a little beer;
And quickly did return
  To say there was none there.

WHY MAY NOT I LOVE JOHNNY?

Johnny shall have a new bonnet,
　And Johnny shall go to the fair,
And Johnny shall have a blue ribbon
　To tie up his bonny brown hair.

And why may not I love Johnny?
　And why may not Johnny
　　love me?
And why may not I love Johnny
　As well as another body?

And here's a leg for a stocking,
　And here's a foot for a shoe,
And he has a kiss for his daddy,
　And two for his mammy, I trow.

And why may not I love Johnny?
　And why may not Johnny love
　　me?
And why may not I love Johnny
　As well as another body?

JACK JELF

Little Jack Jelf
Was put on the shelf
Because he could not spell "pie";
　When his aunt, Mrs. Grace,
　Saw his sorrowful face,
She could not help saying, "Oh, fie!"

And since Master Jelf
Was put on the shelf
Because he could not spell "pie,"
　Let him stand there so grim,
　And no more about him,
For I wish him a very good-bye!

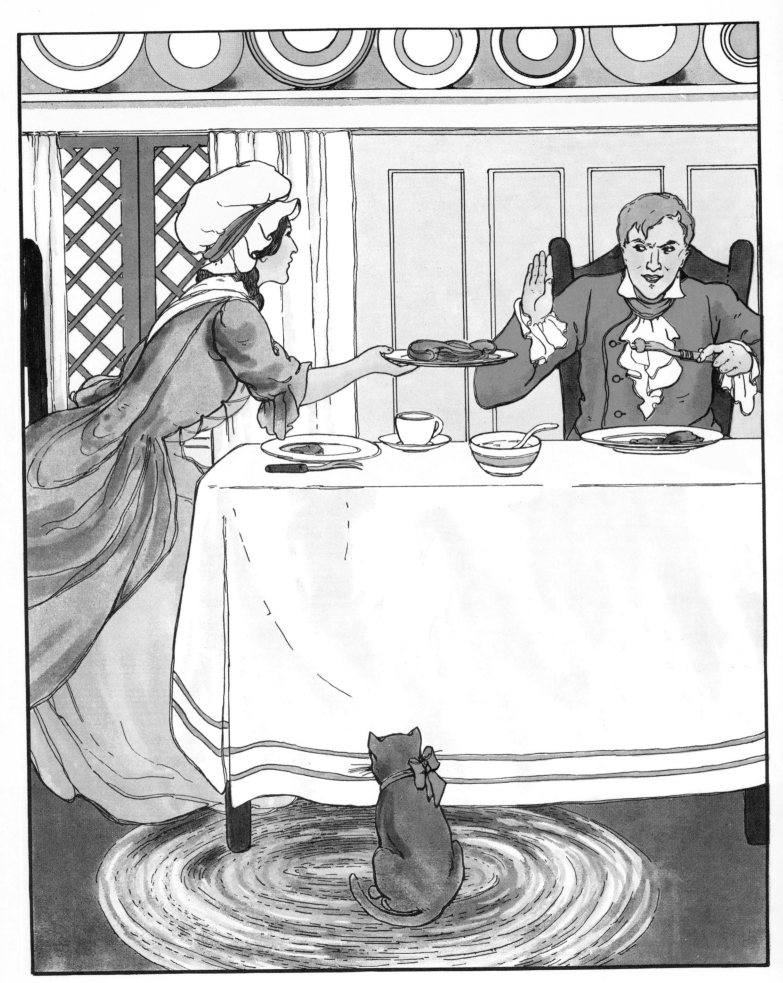

JACK SPRAT

JACK SPRAT

Jack Sprat
Could eat no fat,
His wife could eat no lean;
And so,
Betwixt them both,
They licked the platter clean.

HUSH-A-BYE

Hush-a-bye, baby,
Daddy is near;
Mamma is a lady,
And that's very clear.

DAFFODILS

Daffy-down-dilly has come to town
In a yellow petticoat and a green
gown.

THE GIRL IN THE LANE

The girl in the lane, that couldn't
speak plain,
Cried, "Gobble, gobble, gobble":
The man on the hill that couldn't
stand still,
Went hobble hobble, hobble.

HUSH-A-BYE

Hush-a-bye, baby, lie still with thy
daddy,
Thy mammy has gone to the
mill,
To get some meal to bake a cake,
So pray, my dear baby, lie still.

NANCY DAWSON

Nancy Dawson was so fine
She wouldn't get up to serve the
swine;
She lies in bed till eight or
nine,
So it's Oh, poor Nancy Dawson.

And do ye ken Nancy Dawson,
honey?
The wife who sells the barley, honey?
She won't get up to feed her swine,
And do ye ken Nancy Dawson,
honey?

HANDY PANDY

Handy Pandy, Jack-a-dandy,
Loves plum cake and sugar candy.
He bought some at a grocer's shop,
And out he came, hop, hop, hop!

JACK AND JILL

Jack and Jill went up the hill,
　To fetch a pail of water;
Jack fell down, and broke his crown,
　And Jill came tumbling after.

Then up Jack got and off did trot,
　As fast as he could caper,
To old Dame Dob, who patched his
　　nob
　With vinegar and brown paper.

THE ALPHABET

A, B, C, and D,
Pray, playmates, agree.
E, F, and G,
Well, so it shall be.
J, K, and L,
In peace we will dwell.
M, N, and O,
To play let us go.
P, Q, R, and S,
Love may we possess.
W, X, and Y,
Will not quarrel or die.
Z, and ampersand,
Go to school at command.

DANCE TO YOUR DADDIE

Dance to your daddie,
My bonnie laddie;
Dance to your daddie, my bonnie
  lamb;
You shall get a fishy,
On a little dishy;
You shall get a fishy, when the boat
  comes home.

ONE MISTY MOISTY MORNING

One misty moisty morning,
  When cloudy was the weather,
I chanced to meet an old man,
  Clothed all in leather.
He began to compliment
  And I began to grin.
How do you do? And how do you do?
  And how do you do again?

ROBIN HOOD AND LITTLE JOHN

Robin Hood, Robin Hood,
  Is in the mickle wood!
Little John, Little John,
  He to the town is gone.

Robin Hood, Robin Hood,
  Telling his beads,
All in the greenwood
  Among the green weeds.
Little John, Little John,
  If he comes no more,
Robin Hood, Robin Hood,
  We shall fret full sore!

RAIN

Rain, rain, go to Spain,
And never come back again.

ROBIN HOOD

THE ROBINS

A robin and a robin's son
Once went to town to buy a bun.
They couldn't decide on plum or
    plain,
And so they went back home again.

THE OLD MAN

There was an old man
In a velvet coat,
He kissed a maid
And gave her a groat.
The groat it was crack'd
And would not go,—
Ah, old man, do you serve me so?

THE OLD WOMAN FROM FRANCE

There came an old woman from
    France
Who taught grown-up children to
    dance;
    But they were so stiff,
    She sent them home in a sniff,
This sprightly old woman from
    France.

TEETH AND GUMS

Thirty white horses upon a red hill,
Now they tramp, now they champ,
    now they stand still.

IF ALL THE SEAS WERE ONE SEA

If all the seas were one sea,
What a *great* sea that would be!
And if all the trees were one tree,
What a *great* tree that would be!
And if all the axes were one axe,
What a *great* axe that would be!
And if all the men were one man,
What a *great* man he would be!
And if the *great* man took the *great*
    axe,
And cut down the *great* tree,
And let it fall into the *great* sea,
What a splish splash *that* would be!

T'OTHER LITTLE TUNE

I won't be my father's Jack,
  I won't be my father's Jill;
I will be the fiddler's wife,
  And have music when I will.
      T'other little tune,
      T'other little tune,
      Prithee, Love, play me
      T'other little tune.

MY KITTEN

Hey, my kitten, my kitten,
  And hey, my kitten, my deary!
Such a sweet pet as this
  Was neither far nor neary.

HERE SITS THE LORD MAYOR

FOREHEAD, EYES, CHEEKS, NOSE, MOUTH, AND CHIN

Here sits the Lord Mayor,
　　Here sit his two men,
Here sits the cock,
　　Here sits the hen,
Here sit the little chickens,
　　Here they run in.
Chin-chopper, chin-chopper, chin chopper, chin!

TWO PIGEONS

I had two pigeons bright and gay,
They flew from me the other day.
What was the reason they did go?
I cannot tell, for I do not know.

PANCAKE DAY

Great A, little a,
This is pancake day;
Toss the ball high,
Throw the ball low,
Those that come after
May sing heigh-ho!

A PLUM PUDDING

Flour of England, fruit of Spain,
　　Met together in a shower of rain;
Put in a bag tied round with a
　　string;
If you'll tell me this riddle,
I'll give you a ring.

A SURE TEST

If you are to be a gentleman,
    As I suppose you'll be,
You'll neither laugh nor smile,
    For a tickling of the knee.

LOCK AND KEY

"I am a gold lock."

"I am a gold key."

"I am a silver lock."

"I am a silver key."

"I am a brass lock."

"I am a brass key."

"I am a lead lock."

"I am a lead key."

"I am a don lock."

"I am a don key!"

THE LION AND THE UNICORN

The Lion and the Unicorn were
    fighting for the crown,
The Lion beat the Unicorn all
    around the town.
Some gave them white bread, and
    some gave them brown,
Some gave them plum-cake, and
    sent them out of town.

THE MERCHANTS OF LONDON

Hey diddle dinkety poppety pet,
The merchants of London they wear
    scarlet,
Silk in the collar and gold in the
    hem,
So merrily march the merchant
    men.

I HAD A LITTLE HUSBAND

I had a little husband no bigger
    than my thumb,
I put him in a pint pot, and there
    I bid him drum,
I bought a little handkerchief to
    wipe his little nose,
And a pair of little garters to tie his
    little hose.

TO BABYLON

How many miles is it to Babylon?—
    Threescore miles and ten.
Can I get there by candle-light?—
    Yes, and back again.
If your heels are nimble and light,
You may get there by candle-light.

I'LL TELL YOU A STORY

I'll tell you a story
    About Jack-a-Nory:
And now my story's begun.
I'll tell you another
    About his brother:
And now my story is done.

A STRANGE OLD WOMAN

There was an old woman, and what
    do you think?
She lived upon nothing but victuals
    and drink;
Victuals and drink were the chief
    of her diet,
And yet this old woman could
    never be quiet.

BAA, BAA, BLACK SHEEP

Baa, baa, black sheep,
Have you any wool?
Yes, marry, have I,
Three bags full;

One for my master,
One for my dame,
But none for the little boy
Who cries in the lane.

LITTLE FRED

When little Fred went to bed,
He always said his prayers;
He kissed mamma, and then papa,
And straightway went upstairs.

SLEEP, BABY, SLEEP

Sleep, baby, sleep,
Our cottage vale is deep:
The little lamb is on the green,
With woolly fleece so soft and clean—
Sleep, baby, sleep.

Sleep, baby, sleep,
Down where the woodbines creep;
Be always like the lamb so mild,
A kind, and sweet, and gentle child.
Sleep, baby, sleep.

CRY, BABY

Cry, baby, cry,
Put your finger in your eye,
And tell your mother it wasn't I.

BAA, BAA, BLACK SHEEP

THE CAT AND THE FIDDLE

Hey, diddle, diddle!
The cat and the fiddle,
The cow jumped over the moon;
The little dog laughed
To see such sport,
And the dish ran away with the spoon.

DOCTOR FELL

I do not like thee, Doctor Fell;
The reason why I cannot tell;
But this I know, and know full well,
I do not like thee, Doctor Fell!

A COUNTING-OUT RHYME

Hickery, dickery, 6 and 7,
Alabone, Crackabone, 10 and 11,
Spin, spun, muskidun,
Twiddle 'em, twaddle 'em, 21.

JACK AND HIS FIDDLE

"Jacky, come and give me thy fiddle,
　If ever thou mean to thrive."
"Nay, I'll not give my fiddle
　To any man alive.

"If I should give my fiddle,
　They'll think that I've gone mad;
For many a joyous day
　My fiddle and I have had."

BUTTONS

　Buttons, a farthing a pair!
Come, who will buy them of me?
They're round and sound and pretty,
And fit for girls of the city.
Come, who will buy them of me?
　Buttons, a farthing a pair!

HOT BOILED BEANS

Ladies and gentlemen come to
　supper—
Hot boiled beans and very good
　butter.

When the pie was opened
  The birds began to sing;
Was not that a dainty dish
  To set before the king?

The king was in his counting-house,
  Counting out his money;
The queen was in the parlor,
  Eating bread and honey.

The maid was in the garden,
  Hanging out the clothes;
When down came a blackbird
  And snapped off her nose.

LITTLE PUSSY

I like little Pussy,
  Her coat is so warm,
And if I don't hurt her
  She'll do me no harm;
So I'll not pull her tail,
  Nor drive her away,
But Pussy and I
  Very gently will play.

SING A SONG OF SIXPENCE

Sing a song of sixpence,
  A pocket full of rye;
Four-and-twenty blackbirds
  Baked in a pie!

SING A SONG OF SIXPENCE

The horns that grew on his head, sir,
    they were so wondrous high,
As I've been plainly told, sir, they
    reached up to the sky.
  The sky, the sky, the sky;
As I've been plainly told, sir, they
    reached up to the sky.

The tail that grew from his back, sir,
    was six yards and an ell;
And it was sent to Derby to toll the
    market bell;
  The bell, the bell, the bell;
And it was sent to Derby to toll
    the market bell.

TOMMY TITTLEMOUSE

Little Tommy Tittlemouse
Lived in a little house;
He caught fishes
In other men's ditches.

THE DERBY RAM

As I was going to Derby all on a
    market-day,
I met the finest ram, sir, that ever
    was fed upon hay;
  Upon hay, upon hay, upon hay;
I met the finest ram, sir, that ever
    was fed upon hay.
This ram was fat behind, sir; this
    ram was fat before;
This ram was ten yards round, sir;
    indeed, he was no more;
  No more, no more, no more;
This ram was ten yards round, sir;
    indeed, he was no more.

This is the way we wash our clothes,
On a cold and frosty morning.

This is the way we go to school,
Go to school, go to school,
This is the way we go to school,
On a cold and frosty morning.

This is the way we come out of school,
Come out of school, come out of
    school,
This is the way we come out of
    school,
On a cold and frosty morning.

THE HOBBY-HORSE

I had a little hobby-horse,
    And it was dapple gray;
Its head was made of pea-straw,
    Its tail was made of hay.

I sold it to an old woman
    For a copper groat;
And I'll not sing my song again
    Without another coat.

THE MULBERRY BUSH

Here we go round the mulberry bush,
The mulberry bush, the mulberry
    bush,
Here we go round the mulberry bush.
On a cold and frosty morning.

This is the way we wash our hands,
Wash our hands, wash our hands,
This is the way we wash our hands,
On a cold and frosty morning.

This is the way we wash our clothes.
Wash our clothes, wash our clothes,

YOUNG LAMBS TO SELL

If I'd as much money as I could tell,
I never would cry young lambs to sell;
Young lambs to sell, young lambs to sell;
I never would cry young lambs to sell.

OLD WOMAN, OLD WOMAN

There was an old woman tossed in
    a basket,
    Seventeen times as high as the
      moon;
But where she was going no mortal
    could tell,
    For under her arm she carried a
      broom.
"Old woman, old woman, old
    woman," said I,
    "Whither, oh whither, oh whither
    so high?"
"To sweep the cobwebs from the sky;
    And I'll be with you by-and-by."

THE FIRST OF MAY

The fair maid who, the first of May,
Goes to the fields at break of day,
And washes in dew from the haw-
    thorn-tree,
Will ever after handsome be.

BOY AND THE SPARROW

A little cock-sparrow sat on a green
    tree,
And he chirruped, he chirruped, so
    merry was he;
A naughty boy came with his wee
    bow and arrow,
Determined to shoot this little cock-
    sparrow.
"This little cock-sparrow shall make
    me a stew,
And his giblets shall make me a
    little pie, too."
"Oh, no," says the sparrow "I won't
    make a stew."
So he flapped his wings and away
    he flew.

THE OLD WOMAN TOSSED IN A BASKET

SULKY SUE

Here's Sulky Sue,
What shall we do?
Turn her face to the wall
Till she comes to.

THE HOUSE THAT
JACK BUILT

This is the house that Jack built.
This is the malt
That lay in the house that Jack
    built.

This is the rat,
That ate the malt
That lay in the house that Jack
    built.

This is the cat,
That killed the rat,

That ate the malt
That lay in the house that Jack
    built.

This is the dog,
That worried the cat,
That killed the rat,
That ate the malt
That lay in the house that Jack
    built.

This is the cow with the crumpled
    horn,
That tossed the dog,
That worried the cat,
That killed the rat,
That ate the malt
That lay in the house that Jack
    built.

This is the maiden all forlorn,
That milked the cow with the
    crumpled horn,
That tossed the dog,
That worried the cat,
That killed the rat,
That ate the malt
That lay in the house that Jack
    built.

This is the man all tattered and
    torn,
That kissed the maiden all forlorn,
That milked the cow with the
    crumpled horn,
That tossed the dog,
That worried the cat,
That killed the rat,

That ate the malt

That lay in the house that Jack
  built.

This is the priest all shaven and
  shorn,

That married the man all tattered
  and torn,

That kissed the maiden all forlorn,

That milked the cow with the
  crumpled horn,

That tossed the dog,

That worried the cat,

That killed the rat,

That ate the malt

That lay in the house that Jack
  built.

This is the cock that crowed in the
  morn,

That waked the priest all shaven
  and shorn,

That married the man all tattered
  and torn,

That kissed the maiden all forlorn,

That milked the cow with the
  crumpled horn,

That tossed the dog,

That worried the cat,

That killed the rat,

That ate the malt

That lay in the house that Jack
  built.

This is the farmer sowing the corn,

That kept the cock that crowed in
  the morn.

That waked the priest all shaven
  and shorn,

That married the man all tattered
  and torn,

That kissed the maiden all forlorn,

That milked the cow with the
  crumpled horn,

That tossed the dog,

That worried the cat,

That killed the rat,

That ate the malt

That lay in the house that Jack built.

SATURDAY, SUNDAY

On Saturday night
    Shall be all my care
To powder my locks
    And curl my hair.

On Sunday morning
    My love will come in,
When he will marry me
    With a gold ring.

THE OLD WOMAN AND THE PEDLAR

LITTLE JENNY WREN

Little Jenny Wren fell sick,
    Upon a time;
In came Robin Redbreast
    And brought her cake and
        wine.

"Eat well of my cake, Jenny,
    Drink well of my wine."
"Thank you, Robin, kindly,
    You shall be mine."

Jenny she got well,
    And stood upon her feet,
And told Robin plainly
    She loved him not a bit.

Robin being angry,
    Hopped upon a twig,
Saying, "Out upon you! Fie upon
        you!
    Bold-faced jig!"

THE OLD WOMAN AND
THE PEDLAR

There was an old woman, as I've
    heard tell,
She went to market her eggs for to
    sell;
She went to market all on a market-
    day,
And she fell asleep on the King's
    highway.

There came by a pedlar whose
    name was Stout,
He cut her petticoats all round
    about;
He cut her petticoats up to the
    knees,
Which made the old woman to shiver
    and freeze.

When the little old woman first did
    wake,
She began to shiver and she began
    to shake;
She began to wonder and she began
    to cry,
"Lauk a mercy on me, this can't
    be I!

"But if it be I, as I hope it be,
I've a little dog at home, and he'll
  know me;
If it be I, he'll wag his little tail,
And if it be not I, he'll loudly bark
  and wail."

Home went the little woman all in
  the dark;
Up got the little dog, and he began
  to bark;
He began to bark, so she began to
  cry,
"Lauk a mercy on me, this is none
  of I!"

BOBBY SNOOKS

Little Bobby Snooks was fond of
  his books,
  And loved by his usher and master;
But naughty Jack Spry, he got a
  black eye,
  And carries his nose in a plaster.

THE LITTLE MOPPET

I had a little moppet,
I put it in my pocket,
And fed it with corn and hay.
  There came a proud beggar.
  And swore he should have her;
And stole my little moppet away.

I SAW A SHIP A-SAILING

I saw a ship a-sailing,
A-sailing on the sea;
And, oh! it was all laden
With pretty things for thee!

There were comfits in the cabin,
And apples in the hold;
The sails were made of silk,
And the masts were made of gold.

The four-and-twenty sailors
That stood between the decks,
Were four-and-twenty white mice
With chains about their necks.

The captain was a duck,
With a packet on his back;
And when the ship began to move,
The captain said, "Quack! Quack!"

A WALNUT

As soft as silk, as white as milk,
As bitter as gall, a strong wall,
And a green coat covers me all.

THE MAN IN THE MOON

The Man in the Moon came tumbling
  down,
  And asked the way to Norwich;
He went by the south, and burnt his
  mouth
  With eating cold pease porridge.

ONE, HE LOVES

One, he loves; two, he loves;
Three, he loves, they say;
Four, he loves with all his heart;
Five, he casts away.
Six, he loves; seven, she loves;
Eight, they both love.
Nine, he comes; ten, he tarries;
Eleven, he courts; twelve, he mar-
  ries.

BAT, BAT

Bat, bat,
Come under my hat,
And I'll give you a slice of bacon;
  And when I bake
  I'll give you a cake
If I am not mistaken.

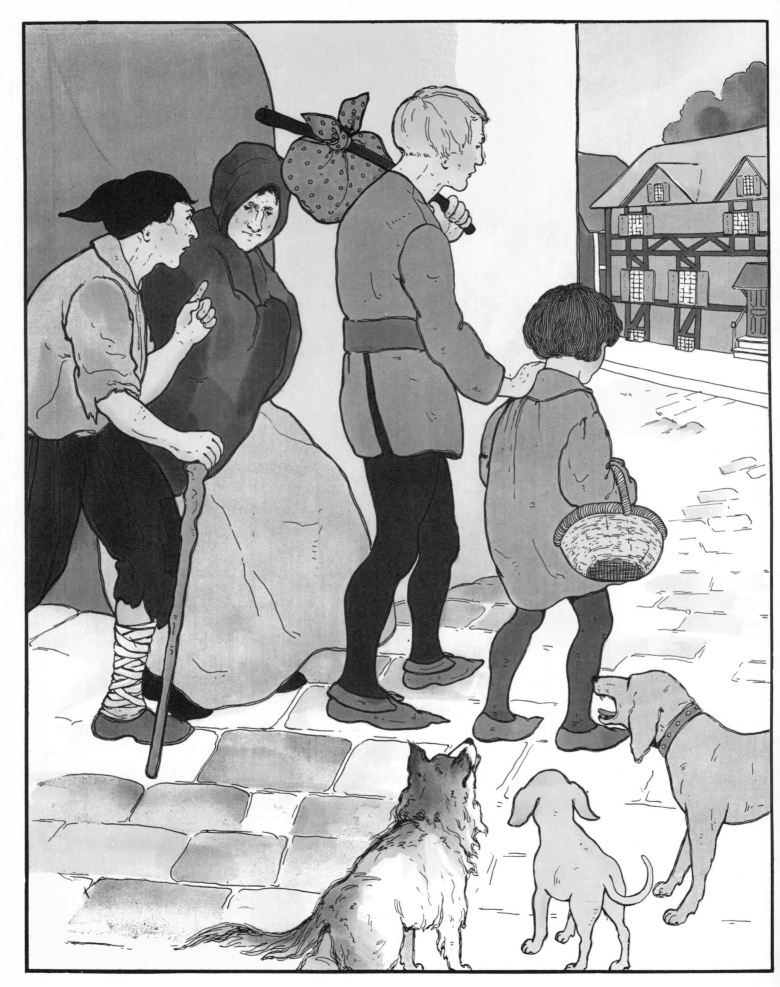

HARK! HARK! THE DOGS DO BARK!

MY LOVE

Saw ye aught of my love a-coming
   from the market?
  A peck of meal upon her back,
  A babby in her basket;
Saw ye aught of my love a-coming
   from the market?

THE MAN OF BOMBAY

There was a fat man of Bombay,

Who was smoking one sunshiny day;

  When a bird called a snipe

  Flew away with his pipe,

Which vexed the fat man of Bombay

HARK! HARK!

Hark, hark! the dogs do bark!
  Beggars are coming to town:
Some in jags, and some in rags,
  And some in velvet gown.

THE HART

The hart he loves the high wood,
  The hare she loves the hill;
The Knight he loves his bright
   sword,
  The Lady—loves her will.

MY MAID MARY

My maid Mary she minds the dairy,
 While I go a-hoeing and mowing
  each morn;
Gaily run the reel and the little
  spinning wheel.
 While I am singing and mowing
  my corn.

A DIFFICULT RHYME

What is the rhyme for porringer?
The king he had a daughter fair,
And gave the Prince of Orange her.

POOR OLD ROBINSON
CRUSOE!

Poor old Robinson Crusoe!
Poor old Robinson Crusoe!
 They made him a coat
 Of an old Nanny goat.
I wonder why they should do so!
 With a ring-a-ting-tang,
 And a ring-a-ting-tang,
Poor old Robinson Crusoe!

A SIEVE

A riddle, a riddle, as I suppose,
A hundred eyes and never a nose!

PRETTY JOHN WATTS

Pretty John Watts,
We are troubled with rats.
Will you drive them out of the
    house?
We have mice, too, in plenty,
That feast in the pantry,
But let them stay
And nibble away,
What harm in a little brown mouse?

GOOD ADVICE

Come when you're called,
    Do what you're bid,
Shut the door after you,
    And never be chid.

I LOVE SIXPENCE

I love sixpence, a jolly, jolly
    sixpence,
    I love sixpence as my life;
I spent a penny of it, I spent a
    penny of it,
    I took a penny home to my
    wife.

Oh, my little fourpence, a jolly,
    jolly fourpence,
    I love fourpence as my life;
I spent twopence of it, I spent two-
    pence of it,
    And I took twopence home to
    my wife.

BYE, BABY BUNTING

Bye, baby bunting,
Father's gone a-hunting,
Mother's gone a-milking,
Sister's gone a-silking,
And brother's gone to buy a skin
To wrap the baby bunting in.

TOM, TOM, THE PIPER'S SON

Tom, Tom, the piper's son,
Stole a pig, and away he run,
    The pig was eat,
    And Tom was beat,
And Tom ran crying down the
    street.

COMICAL FOLK

In a cottage in Fife
Lived a man and his wife
Who, believe me, were comical folk;
    For, to people's surprise,
    They both saw with their eyes,
And their tongues moved whenever
    they spoke!

When they were asleep,
I'm told, that to keep
Their eyes open they could not
    contrive;
    They both walked on their feet,
    And 'twas thought what they
    eat
Helped, with drinking, to keep them
    alive!

COCK-CROW

Cocks crow in the morn
    To tell us to rise,
And he who lies late
    Will never be wise;
For early to bed
    And early to rise,
Is the way to be healthy
    And wealthy and wise.

TOMMY SNOOKS

As Tommy Snooks and Bessy
    Brooks
    Were walking out one Sunday,
Says Tommy Snooks to Bessy
    Brooks,
    "Wilt marry me on Monday?"

COCK-CROW

THE THREE SONS

There was an old woman had three
    sons,
Jerry and James and John,
Jerry was hanged, James was
    drowned,
John was lost and never was found;
And there was an end of her three
    sons,
Jerry and James and John!

THE BLACKSMITH

"Robert Barnes, my fellow fine,
Can you shoe this horse of mine?"
"Yes, good sir, that I can,
As well as any other man;
There's a nail, and there's a prod,
Now, good sir, your horse is shod."

TWO GRAY KITS

The two gray kits,
And the gray kits' mother,
    All went over
The bridge together.

The bridge broke down,
    They all fell in;
"May the rats go with you,"
    Says Tom Bolin.

ONE, TWO, BUCKLE
MY SHOE

One, two,
Buckle my shoe;
Three, four,
Knock at the door;
Five, six,
Pick up sticks;
Seven, eight,
Lay them straight;
Nine, ten,
A good, fat hen;
Eleven, twelve,
Dig and delve;
Thirteen, fourteen,
Maids a-courting;
Fifteen, sixteen,
Maids in the kitchen;
Seventeen, eighteen,
Maids a-waiting;
Nineteen, twenty,
My plate's empty.

COCK-A-DOODLE-DO!

Cock-a-doodle-do!
My dame has lost her shoe,
My master's lost his fiddle-stick
And knows not what to do.

Cock-a-doodle-do!
What is my dame to do?
Till master finds his fiddle-stick,
She'll dance without her shoe.

PAIRS OR PEARS

Twelve pairs hanging high,
Twelve knights riding by,
Each knight took a pear,
And yet left a dozen there.

BELLEISLE

At the siege of Belleisle
I was there all the while,
All the while, all the while,
At the siege of Belleisle.

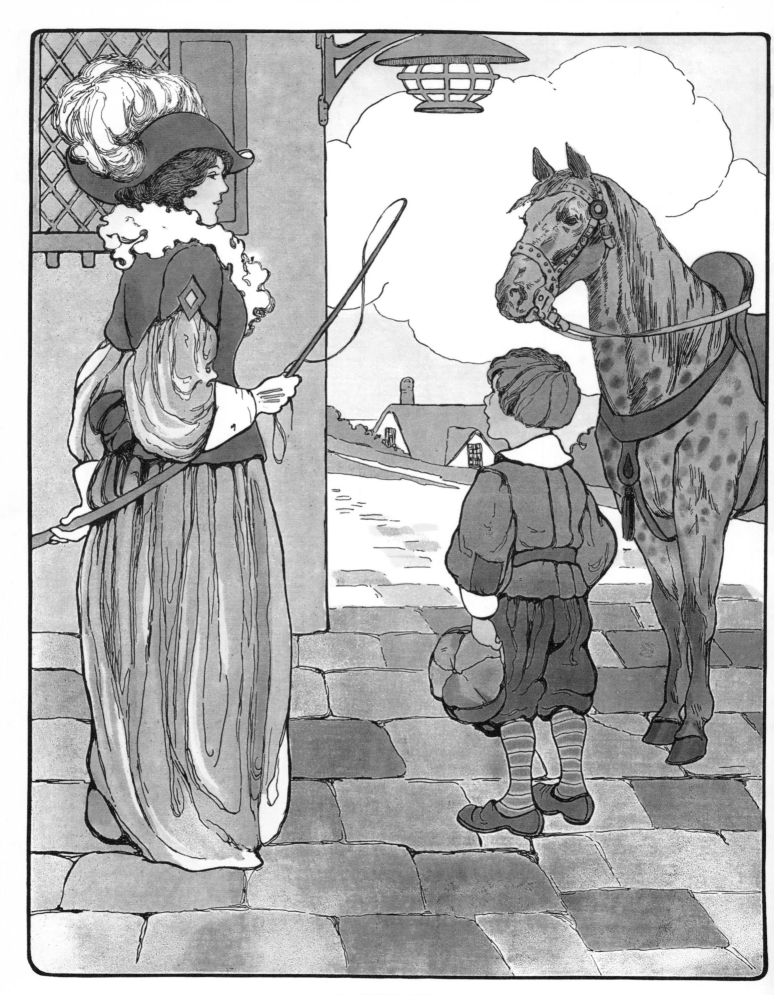

DAPPLE-GRAY

OLD KING COLE

Old King Cole
Was a merry old soul,
And a merry old soul was he;
He called for his pipe,
And he called for his bowl,
And he called for his fiddlers three!
And every fiddler, he had a fine
  fiddle,
And a very fine fiddle had he.
"Twee tweedle dee, tweedle dee,"
  went the fiddlers.
Oh, there's none so rare
As can compare
With King Cole and his fiddlers
  three.

SEE, SEE

See, see! What shall I see?
A horse's head where his tail
  should be.

DAPPLE-GRAY

I had a little pony,
  His name was Dapple-Gray,
I lent him to a lady,
  To ride a mile away.
She whipped him, she slashed him,
  She rode him through the mire;
I would not lend my pony now
  For all the lady's hire.

A WELL

As round as an apple, as deep as a
  cup,
And all the king's horses can't fill
  it up.

COFFEE AND TEA

Molly, my sister and I fell out,
And what do you think it was all
  about?
She loved coffee and I loved tea,
And that was the reason we couldn't
  agree.

PUSSY-CAT MEW

Pussy-cat Mew jumped over a coal,
And in her best petticoat burnt a
  great hole.
Poor Pussy's weeping, she'll have
  no more milk
Until her best petticoat's mended
  with silk.

A COCK AND BULL STORY

The cock's on the housetop blowing
his horn;
The bull's in the barn a-threshing
of corn;
The maids in the meadows are
making of hay;
The ducks in the river are swim-
ming away.

FOR BABY

You shall have an apple,
YOU shall have a plum,
You shall have a rattle,
When papa comes home.

THE LITTLE GIRL WITH A CURL

There was a little girl who had a little
curl
Right in the middle of her forehead;
When she was good, she was very,
very good,
And when she was bad she was
horrid.

DREAMS

Friday night's dream, on Saturday
told,
Is sure to come true, be it never so
old.

OVER THE WATER

Over the water, and over the sea,
And over the water to Charley,
I'll have none of your nasty beef,
Nor I'll have none of your barley;
But I'll have some of your very best
    flour
To make a white cake for my
    Charley.

CANDLE-SAVING

To make your candles last for aye,
You wives and maids give ear-O!
To put them out's the only way,
Says honest John Boldero.

MYSELF

As I walked by myself,
And talked to myself,
    Myself said unto me:
"Look to thyself,
Take care of thyself,
    For nobody cares for thee."

I answered myself,
And said to myself
    In the selfsame repartee:
"Look to thyself,
Or not look to thyself,
    The selfsame thing will be."

LADYBIRD

OLD GRIMES

Old Grimes is dead, that good old
man,
We ne'er shall see him more;
He used to wear a long brown coat
All buttoned down before.

A WEEK OF BIRTHDAYS

Monday's child is fair of face,
Tuesday's child is full of grace,
Wednesday's child is full of woe,
Thursday's child has far to go,
Friday's child is loving and giving,
Saturday's child works hard for its
living,
But the child that's born on the
Sabbath day
Is bonny and blithe, and good and
gay.

FEARS AND TEARS

Tommy's tears and Mary's fears
Will make them old before their
years.

THE KILKENNY CATS

There were once two cats of
Kilkenny.
Each thought there was one cat too
many;
So they fought and they fit,
And they scratched and they bit,
Till, excepting their nails,
And the tips of their tails,
Instead of two cats, there weren't
any.

A CHIMNEY

Black within and red without;
Four corners round about.

LADYBIRD

Ladybird, ladybird, fly away home!
Your house is on fire, your children
all gone,
All but one, and her name is Ann,
And she crept under the pudding
pan.

THE MAN WHO HAD NAUGHT

There was a man and he had naught,
    And robbers came to rob him;
He crept up to the chimney pot,
    And then they thought they
      had him.

But he got down on t'other side,
    And then they could not find
      him;
He ran fourteen miles in fifteen days,
    And never looked behind him.

THE TAILORS AND THE SNAIL

Four and Twenty tailors
    Went to kill a snail;
The best man among them
    Durst not touch her tail;
She put out her horns
    Like a little Kyloe cow.
Run, tailors, run, or
    She'll kill you all e'en now.

AROUND THE GREEN GRAVEL

Around the green gravel the grass
    grows green,
And all the pretty maids are plain
    to be seen;
Wash them with milk, and clothe
    them with silk,
And write their names with a pen
    and ink.

INTERY, MINTERY

Intery, mintery, cutery corn,
Apple seed and apple thorn;
Wire, brier, limber-lock,
Five geese in a flock,
Sit and sing by a spring,
O-u-t, and in again.

CAESAR'S SONG

Bow-wow-wow!
Whose dog art thou?
Little Tom Tinker's dog,
Bow-wow-wow!

AS I WAS GOING ALONG

As I was going along, along,
A-singing a comical song, song, song,
The lane that I went was so long,
    long, long,
And the song that I sang was so
    long, long, long,
And so I went singing along.

HECTOR PROTECTOR

Hector Protector was dressed all in
    green;
Hector Protector was sent to the
    Queen.
The Queen did not like him,
No more did the King;
So Hector Protector was sent back
    again.

BILLY, BILLY

"Billy, Billy, come and play,
While the sun shines bright as day."

"Yes, my Polly, so I will,
For I love to please you still."

"Billy, Billy, have you seen
Sam and Betsy on the green?"

"Yes, my Poll, I saw them pass,
Skipping o'er the new-mown grass."

"Billy, Billy, come along,
And I will sing a pretty song."

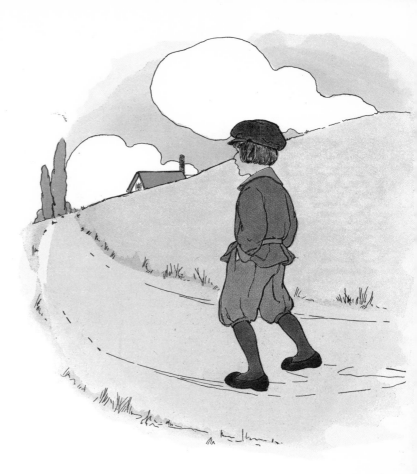

ROCK-A-BYE, BABY

Rock-a-bye, baby, thy cradle is green;
Father's a nobleman, mother's a
    queen;
And Betty's a lady, and wears a
    gold ring;
And Johnny's a drummer, and
    drums for the king.

THE MAN IN THE WILDERNESS

The man in the wilderness
    Asked me
How many strawberries
    Grew in the sea.
I answered him
    As I thought good,
As many as red herrings
    Grew in the wood.

LITTLE JACK HORNER

Little Jack Horner
Sat in the corner,
    Eating of Christmas pie:
He put in his thumb,
And pulled out a plum,
    And said, "What a good boy
      am I!"

THE BIRD SCARER

Away, birds, away!
Take a little and leave a little,
And do not come again;
For if you do,
I will shoot you through,
And there will be an end of you.

MARY, MARY, QUITE CONTRARY

Mary, Mary, quite contrary,
    How does your garden grow?
Silver bells and cockle-shells,
    And pretty maids all of a row.

BESSY BELL AND MARY GRAY

Bessy Bell and Mary Gray,
    They were two bonny lasses;
They built their house upon the lea,
    And covered it with rushes.

Bessy kept the garden gate,
    And Mary kept the pantry;
Bessy always had to wait,
    While Mary lived in plenty.

MARY, MARY, QUITE CONTRARY

DANCE, THUMBKIN DANCE

Dance, Thumbkin, dance;
(keep the thumb in motion
Dance, ye merrymen, everyone.
(all the fingers in motion
For Thumbkin, he can dance alone,
(the thumb alone moving
Thumbkin, he can dance alone.
(the thumb alone moving
Dance, Foreman, dance,
(the first finger moving
Dance, ye merrymen, everyone.
(all moving
But Foreman, he can dance alone,
(the first finger moving
Foreman, he can dance alone.
(the first finger moving
Dance, Longman, dance,
(the second finger moving
Dance, ye merrymen, everyone.
(all moving
For Longman, he can dance alone,
(the second finger moving
Longman, he can dance alone.
(the second finger moving
Dance, Ringman, dance,
(the third finger moving
Dance, ye merrymen, dance.
(all moving
But Ringman cannot dance alone,
(the third finger moving
Ringman, he cannot dance alone.
(the third finger moving
Dance, Littleman, dance,
(the fourth finger moving
Dance, ye merrymen, dance.
(all moving
But Littleman, he can dance alone,
(the fourth finger moving
Littleman, he can dance alone.
(the fourth finger moving

NEEDLES AND PINS

Needles and pins, needles and pins,
When a man marries his trouble
begins.

PUSSY-CAT AND THE DUMPLINGS

Pussy-cat ate the dumplings, the
dumplings,
Pussy-cat ate the dumplings.
Mamma stood by, and cried, "Oh,
fie!
Why did you eat the dump-
lings?"

THE LITTLE BIRD

Once I saw a little bird
　　Come hop, hop, hop;
So I cried, "Little bird,
　　Will you stop, stop, stop?"

And was going to the window
　　To say, "How do you do?"
But he shook his little tail,
　　And far away he flew.

BIRDS OF A FEATHER

Birds of a feather flock together,
　　And so will pigs and swine;
Rats and mice will have their choice,
　　And so will I have mine.

MARY'S CANARY

Mary had a pretty bird,
　　Feathers bright and yellow,
Slender legs—upon my word
　　He was a pretty fellow!

The sweetest note he always sung,
　　Which much delighted Mary.
She often, where the cage was hung,
　　Sat hearing her canary.

THE DUSTY MILLER

Margaret wrote a letter,
Sealed it with her finger,
Threw it in the dam
For the dusty miller.
Dusty was his coat,
Dusty was the siller,
Dusty was the kiss
I'd from the dusty miller.
If I had my pockets
Full of gold and siller,
I would give it all
To my dusty miller.

A STAR

Higher than a house, higher
    than a tree.
Oh! whatever can that be?

THE GREEDY MAN

The greedy man is he who sits
    And bites bits out of plates,
Or else takes up an almanac
    And gobbles all the dates.

THE TEN O'CLOCK
SCHOLAR

A diller, a dollar, a ten o'clock scholar!
    What makes you come so soon?
You used to come at ten o'clock,
    But now you come at noon.

94

THE TEN O'CLOCK SCHOLAR

COCK-A-DOODLE-DO

Oh, my pretty cock, oh, my handsome cock,
I pray you, do not crow before day,
And your comb shall be made of the very
beaten gold,
And your wings of the silver so gray.

AN ICICLE

Lives in winter,
Dies in summer,
And grows with its roots upward!

A SHIP'S NAIL

Over the water,
And under the water,
And always with its head down.

THE OLD WOMAN OF LEEDS

There was an old woman of Leeds,
Who spent all her time in good
 deeds;
  She worked for the poor
  Till her fingers were sore,
This pious old woman of Leeds!

THE BOY IN THE BARN

A little boy went into a barn,
  And lay down on some hay.
An owl came out, and flew about,
  And the little boy ran away.

SUNSHINE

Hick-a-more, Hack-a-more,
On the King's kitchen door,
All the King's horses,
And all the King's men,
Couldn't drive Hick-a-more,
    Hack-a-more,
Off the King's kitchen door.

WILLY, WILLY

Willy, Willy Wilkin
Kissed the maids a-milking,
    Fa, la, la!
And with his merry daffing
He set them all a-laughing,
    Ha, ha, ha!

THE QUARREL

My little old man and I fell out;
I'll tell you what 'twas all about,—
I had money and he had none,
And that's the way the noise begun.

THE PUMPKIN-EATER

Peter, Peter, pumpkin-eater,
Had a wife and couldn't keep her;
He put her in a pumpkin shell,
And there he kept her very well.

TONGS

Long legs, crooked thighs,
Little head, and no eyes.

JACK JINGLE

Little Jack Jingle,
He used to live single;
But when he got tired of this
kind of life,
He left off being single and
lived with his wife.
Now what do you think of
little Jack Jingle?
Before he was married he used
to live single.

PETER, PETER, PUMPKIN-EATER

THAT'S ALL

There was an old woman sat spinning,
And that's the first beginning;

She had a calf,
And that's half;

She took it by the tail,
And threw it over the wall,
And that's all!

SHOEING

Shoe the colt,
Shoe the colt,
Shoe the wild mare;
Here a nail,
There a nail,
Yet she goes bare.

BETTY BLUE

Little Betty Blue
Lost her holiday shoe;
What shall little Betty do?
Give her another
To match the other
And then she'll walk upon two.

BEDTIME

The Man in the Moon looked
    out of the moon,
Looked out of the moon
    and said,
"'Tis time for all children
    on the earth
To think about getting to bed!"

DANCE, LITTLE BABY

Dance, little Baby, dance up high!
Never mind, Baby, Mother is by.
Crow and caper, caper and crow,
There, little Baby, there you go!
Up to the ceiling, down to the
    ground,
Backwards and forwards, round
    and round;
Dance, little Baby and Mother
    will sing,
With the merry coral, ding, ding,
    ding!

MY LITTLE MAID

High diddle doubt, my candle's
    out
    My little maid is not at home;
Saddle my hog and bridle my
    dog,
    And fetch my little maid
    home.

FOR WANT OF A NAIL

For want of a nail, the shoe was lost;
For want of the shoe, the horse was
    lost;
For want of the horse, the rider was
    lost;
For want of the rider, the battle was
    lost;
For want of the battle, the kingdom
    was lost,
And all for the want of a horseshoe
    nail.

THE CROOKED SIXPENCE

There was a crooked man, and he went a crooked mile,
He found a crooked sixpence beside a crooked stile;
He bought a crooked cat, which caught a crooked mouse,
And they all lived together in a little crooked house.

THIS IS THE WAY

This is the way the ladies ride,
　Tri, tre, tre, tree,
　Tri, tre, tre, tree!
This is the way the ladies ride,
　Tri, tre, tre, tre, tri-tre-tre-tree!

This is the way the gentlemen ride,
　Gallop-a-trot,
　Gallop-a-trot!
This is the way the gentlemen ride,
　Gallop-a-gallop-a-trot!

This is the way the farmers ride,
　Hobbledy-hoy,
　Hobbledy-hoy!
This is the way the farmers ride,
　Hobbledy-hobbledy-hoy!

PEASE PORRIDGE

Pease porridge hot,
　Pease porridge cold,
Pease porridge in the pot,
　Nine days old.
Some like it hot,
　Some like it cold,
Some like it in the pot,
　Nine days old.

RING A RING O' ROSES

Ring a ring o' roses,
A pocketful of posies.
Tisha! Tisha!
We all fall down.

PEASE PORRIDGE HOT

DUCKS AND DRAKES

A duck and a drake,
  And a halfpenny cake,
With a penny to pay the old baker.

A hop and a scotch
  Is another notch,
Slitherum, slatherum, take her.

THE DONKEY

Donkey, donkey, old and gray,
Ope your mouth and gently bray;
Lift your ears and blow your horn,
To wake the world this sleepy
    morn.

IF

If all the world were apple pie,
  And all the sea were ink,
And all the trees were bread and
    cheese,
  What should we have for drink?

THE BELLS

"You **owe me five** shillings,"

Say the bells of St. Helen's.

"**W**hen will you pay me?"

Say the bells of Old Bailey.

"When I grow rich,"

Say the bells of Shoreditch.

"When will that be?"

Say the bells of Stepney.

"I do not know,"

Says the great Bell of Bow.

"Two sticks in an apple,"

Ring the bells of Whitechapel.

"Halfpence and farthings,"

Say the bells of St. Martin's.

"Kettles and pans,"

Say the bells of St. Ann's.

"Brickbats and tiles,"

Say the bells of St. Giles.

"Old shoes and slippers,"

Say the bells of St. Peter's.

"Pokers and tongs,"

Say the bells of St. John's.

LITTLE GIRL AND QUEEN

"Little girl, little girl, where have you been?"

"Gathering roses to give to the Queen."

"Little girl, little girl, what gave she you?"

"She gave me a diamond as big as my shoe."

THE KING OF FRANCE

The King of France went up the hill,

With twenty thousand men;

The King of France came down the hill,

And ne'er went up again.

THE TARTS

PETER PIPER

Peter Piper picked a peck of
    pickled peppers;
A peck of pickled peppers Peter
    Piper picked.
If Peter Piper picked a peck of
    pickled peppers,
Where's the peck of pickled peppers
    Peter Piper picked?

ONE TO TEN

1, 2, 3, 4, 5!
I caught a hare alive;
6, 7, 8, 9, 10!
I let her go again.

AN EQUAL

Read my riddle, I pray.
What God never sees,
What the king seldom sees,
What we see every day.

THE TARTS

The Queen of Hearts,
She made some tarts,
All on a summer's day;
The Knave of Hearts,
He stole the tarts,
And took them clean away.

The King of Hearts
Called for the tarts,
And beat the Knave full sore;
The Knave of Hearts
Brought back the tarts,
And vowed he'd steal no more.

WHAT ARE LITTLE BOYS MADE OF?

What are little boys made of, made of?

What are little boys made of?

"Snaps and snails, and puppy-dogs' tails;

And that's what little boys are made of."

What are little girls made of, made of?

What are little girls made of?

"Sugar and spice, and all that's nice;

And that's what little girls are made of."

COME, LET'S TO BED

"To bed! To bed!"
      Says Sleepy-head;
"Tarry awhile," says Slow;
"Put on the pan,"
      Says Greedy Nan;
      "We'll sup before we go."

LITTLE MAID

"Little maid, pretty maid, whither
      goest thou?"
"Down in the forest to milk my
      cow."
'Shall I go with thee?"   "No, not
      now;
When I send for thee, then come
      thou."

So I went into Darlington, that pretty little town,
And there I bought a petticoat, a cloak, and a gown.

I went into the woods and built me a kirk,
And all the birds of the air, they helped me to work.

The hawk with his long claws pulled down the stone,
The dove with her rough bill brought me them home.

The parrot was the clergyman, the peacock was the clerk,
The bullfinch played the organ, — we made merry work.

BANDY LEGS

As I was going to sell my eggs
I met a man with bandy legs,
Bandy legs and crooked toes;
I tripped up his heels, and he
    fell on his nose.

THE GIRL AND THE BIRDS

When I was a little girl, about
    seven years old,
I had n't got a petticoat, to cover
    me from the cold.

A PIG

As I went to Bonner,
I met a pig
Without a wig
Upon my word and honor.

JENNY WREN

As little Jenny Wren
   Was sitting by her shed.
She waggled with her tail,
   And nodded with her head.
She waggled with her tail,
   And nodded with her head,
As little Jenny Wren
   Was sitting by the shed.

LITTLE TOM TUCKER

Little Tom Tucker
   Sings for his supper.
What shall he eat?
   White bread and butter.
How will he cut it
   Without e'er a knife?
How will he be married
   Without e'er a wife?

LITTLE TOM TUCKER

WHERE ARE YOU GOING, MY PRETTY MAID

"Where are you going, my pretty
    maid?"

"I'm going a-milking, sir," she said.

"May I go with you, my pretty
    maid?"

"You're kindly welcome, sir," she
    said.

"What is your father, my pretty
    maid?"

"My father's a farmer, sir," she said.

"What is your fortune, my pretty
    maid?"

"My face is my fortune, sir," she
    said.

"Then I can't marry you, my
    pretty maid."

"Nobody asked you, sir," she said.

THE OLD WOMAN OF GLOUCESTER

There was an old woman of
    Gloucester,

Whose parrot two guineas it cost
    her,
    But its tongue never ceasing,
    Was vastly displeasing

To the talkative woman of
    Gloucester.

MULTIPLICATION IS VEXATION

Multiplication is vexation,
  Division is as bad;
The Rule of Three doth puzzle me,
  And Practice drives me mad.

LITTLE KING BOGGEN

Little King Boggen, he built a fine
  hall,
Pie-crust and pastry-crust, that was
  the wall;
The windows were made of black
  puddings and white,
And slated with pan-cakes,—you
  ne'er saw the like!

WHISTLE

"Whistle, daughter, whistle;
  Whistle, daughter dear."
"I cannot whistle, mammy,
  I cannot whistle clear."
"Whistle, daughter, whistle;
  Whistle for a pound."
"I cannot whistle, mammy,
  I cannot make a sound."

BELL HORSES

Bell horses, bell horses, what
  time of day?
One o'clock, two o'clock, three
  and away.

TAFFY

Taffy was a Welshman, Taffy was
  a thief,
Taffy came to my house and stole a
  piece of beef;
I went to Taffy's house, Taffy was
  not home;
Taffy came to my house and stole a
  marrow-bone.

I went to Taffy's house, Taffy was
  not in;
Taffy came to my house and stole a
  silver pin;
I went to Taffy's house, Taffy was
  in bed,
I took up the marrow-bone and
  flung it at his head.

YOUNG ROGER AND DOLLY

Young Roger came tapping at
    Dolly's window,
    Thumpaty, thumpaty, thump!

He asked for admittance; she
    answered him "No!"
    Frumpaty, frumpaty, frump!

"No, no, Roger, no! as you came
    you may go!"
    Stumpaty, stumpaty, stump!

THE ROBIN

The north wind doth blow,
And we shall have snow,
And what will poor robin do then,
        Poor thing?
He'll sit in a barn,
And keep himself warm,
And hide his head under his wing,
        Poor thing!

THE OLD WOMAN OF HARROW

There was an old woman of
    Harrow,
Who visited in a wheelbarrow;
    And her servant before,
    Knocked loud at each door,
To announce the old woman of
    Harrow.

YOUNG ROGER AND DOLLY

THE COACHMAN

Up at Piccadilly, oh!
　　The coachman takes his stand,
And when he meets a pretty girl
　　He takes her by the hand;
Whip away forever, oh!
　　Drive away so clever, oh!
All the way to Bristol, oh!
　　He drives her four-in-hand.

THERE WAS AN OLD WOMAN

There was an old woman who lived
　　in a shoe.
She had so many children she
　　didn't know what to do.
She gave them some broth without
　　any bread.
She whipped them all soundly and
　　put them to bed.

THE PIPER AND HIS COW

There was a piper had a cow,
　　And he had naught to give her;
He pulled out his pipes and played
　　　　her a tune,
　　And bade the cow consider.

The cow considered very well,
　　And gave the piper a penny,
And bade him play the other tune,
　　"Corn rigs are bonny."

THE MAN OF DERBY

A little old man of Derby,
How do you think he served me?
He took away my bread and cheese,
And that is how he served me.

A THORN

I went to the wood and got it;
I sat me down to look for it
And brought it home because I
    couldn't find it.

THE OLD WOMAN OF
SURREY

There was an old woman in Surrey,
Who was morn, noon, and night
    in a hurry;
    Called her husband a fool,
    Drove the children to school,
The worrying old woman of Surrey.

THE LITTLE MOUSE

I have seen you, little mouse,
Running all about the house,
Through the hole your little eye
In the wainscot peeping sly,
Hoping soon some crumbs to steal,
To make quite a hearty meal.

Look before you venture out,
See if pussy is about.
If she's gone, you'll quickly run
To the larder for some fun;
Round about the dishes creep,
Taking into each a peep,
To choose the daintiest that's there,
Spoiling things you do not care.

BOY AND GIRL

There was a little boy and a
    little girl
Lived in an alley;
Says the little boy to the little
    girl,
    "Shall I, oh, shall I?"
Says the little girl to the little
    boy,
    "What shall we do?"
Says the little boy to the little
    girl,
    "I will kiss you."

WHEN

When I was
  a bachelor
I lived by
  myself;
And all the
  bread and
  cheese I got
I laid up on the
  shelf.

The rats and the mice
    They made such a strife,
I was forced to go to London
    To buy me a wife.

The streets were so bad,
    And the lanes were so narrow,
I was forced to bring my wife home
    In a wheelbarrow.

The wheelbarrow broke,
    And my wife had a fall;
Down came wheelbarrow,
    Little wife and all.

WHEN I WAS A BACHELOR

SING, SING

Sing, sing, what shall I
    sing?
Cat's run away with the
    pudding-string!
Do, do, what shall I
    do?
The cat has bitten it
    quite in two.

LONDON BRIDGE

London Bridge is broken down,
Dance over my Lady Lee;
London Bridge is broken down,
With a gay lady.

How shall we build it up again?
Dance over my Lady Lee;
How shall we build it up again?
With a gay lady.

Build it up with silver and gold,
Dance over my Lady Lee;
Build it up with silver and gold,
With a gay lady.

Silver and gold will be stole away,
Dance over my Lady Lee;
Silver and gold will be stole away,
With a gay lady.

Build it up with iron and steel,
Dance over my Lady Lee;
Build it up with iron and steel,
With a gay lady.

Iron and steel will bend and bow,
Dance over my Lady Lee;
Iron and steel will bend and bow,
With a gay lady.

Build it up with wood and clay,
Dance over my Lady Lee;
Build it up with wood and clay,
With a gay lady.

Wood and clay will wash away,
Dance over my Lady Lee;
Wood and clay will wash away,
With a gay lady.

Build it up with stone so strong,
Dance over my Lady Lee;
Huzza! 'twill last for ages long,
With a gay lady.

MARCH WINDS

March winds and April showers
Bring forth May flowers.

THE LOST SHOE

Doodle doodle doo,
The Princess lost her shoe:
  Her Highness hopped,—
  The fiddler stopped,
Not knowing what to do.

HOT CODLINS

There was a little woman, as I've
    been told,
Who was not very young, nor yet
    very old;
Now this little woman her living got
By selling codlins, hot, hot, hot!

THE BALLOON

"What is the news of the day,
Good neighbor, I pray?"
"They say the balloon
Is gone up to the moon!"

A CHERRY

As I went through the garden gap,
Who should I meet but Dick Red-
    cap!
A stick in his hand, a stone in his
    throat,—
If you'll tell me this riddle, I'll
    give you a groat.

121

SWAN

Swan, swan, over the sea;
Swim, swan, swim!
Swan, swan, back again;
Well swum, swan!

THREE STRAWS

Three straws on a staff
Would make a baby cry and laugh.

THE MAN OF TOBAGO

There was an old man of Tobago
Who lived on rice, gruel, and sago,
Till much to his bliss,
His physician said this:
"To a leg, sir, of mutton, you may
go."

DING, DONG, BELL

Ding, dong, bell,
Pussy's in the well!
Who put her in?
Little Tommy Lin.

Who pulled her out?
Little Johnny Stout.
What a naughty boy was that,
To try to drown poor pussy-cat.
Who never did him any harm,
But killed the mice in his father's
barn!

A SUNSHINY SHOWER

A sunshiny shower
Won't last half an hour.

The mischievous raven flew laughing away,
    Bumpety, bumpety, bump!
And vowed he would serve them
    the same the next day,
    Lumpety, lumpety lump!

CHRISTMAS

Christmas is coming, the geese are
    getting fat,
Please to put a penny in an old
    man's hat;
If you haven't got a penny a
    ha'penny will do,
If you haven't got a ha'penny, God
    bless you.

THE FARMER AND THE RAVEN

A farmer went trotting upon his
    gray mare,
    Bumpety, bumpety, bump!
With his daughter behind him so
    rosy and fair,
    Lumpety, lumpety, lump!

A raven cried croak! and they all
    tumbled down,
    Bumpety, bumpety, bump!
The mare broke her knees, and the
    farmer his crown,
    Lumpety, lumpety, lump!

WILLY BOY

"Willy boy, Willy boy, where are
    you going?
I will go with you, if that I
    may."
"I'm going to the meadow to
    see them a-mowing,
I'm going to help them to make
    the hay."

POLLY AND SUKEY

Polly, put the kettle on,
Polly, put the kettle on,
Polly, put the kettle on,
    And let's drink tea.

Sukey, take it off again,
Sukey, take it off again,
Sukey, take it off again,
    They're all gone away.

THE DEATH AND BURIAL OF POOR COCK ROBIN

Who killed Cock Robin?
"I," said the sparrow,
"With my little bow and arrow,
I killed Cock Robin."

Who saw him die?
"I," said the fly,
"With my little eye,
I saw him die."

Who caught his blood?
"I," said the fish,
"With my little dish,
I caught his blood."

Who'll make his shroud?
"I," said the beetle,
"With my thread and needle,
I'll make his shroud."

124

Who'll carry the torch?
"I," said the linnet,
"I'll come in a minute,
I'll carry the torch."

Who'll be the clerk?
"I," said the lark,
"If it's not in the dark,
I'll be the clerk."

Who'll dig his grave?
"I," said the owl,
"With my spade and trowel
I'll dig his grave."

Who'll be the parson?
"I," said the rook,
"With my little book,
I'll be the parson."

Who'll be chief mourner?
"I," said the dove,
"I mourn for my love,
I'll be chief mourner."

Who'll sing a psalm?
"I," said the thrush,
"As I sit in a bush.
I'll sing a psalm."

Who'll carry the coffin?
"I," said the kite,
"If it's not in the night,
I'll carry the coffin."

Who'll toll the bell?
"I," said the bull,
"Because I can pull,
I'll toll the bell."

All the birds of the air
Fell sighing and sobbing,
When they heard the bell toll
For poor Cock Robin.

THE MOUSE AND THE CLOCK

Hickory, dickory, dock!
The mouse ran up the clock;
 The clock struck one,
 And down he run,
Hickory, dickory, dock!

THE BUNCH OF BLUE RIBBONS